The Gold at the End of the Rainbow

For Abbie & Mary
From Poppa & Johnnie & Grandma Paula
(San Francisco - 1998)
Trip

By Wolfram Hänel

Illustrated by Loek Koopmans

Translated by Anthea Bell

North-South Books

New York · London

"May I have some more potatoes?" asked Brendan, pushing his plate across the table.

His grandfather looked out the window. Huge raindrops were splashing against the panes, and the wind was howling outside, rattling the shutters.

"If only we had a pig, that would feed us through the winter," said Grandpa. "And maybe a few chickens. Then we could have eggs and bacon." Grandpa sighed. "Oh, well," he said with a laugh. "We might as well wish for the gold at the end of the rainbow."

"What gold?" asked Brendan.

Grandpa drew his chair close to the flickering fire and took Brendan on his knee.

"At the end of the rainbow," he began, "at the end of the rainbow there is an island. There's a treasure in a huge pot buried on that island. The pot is full of gold pieces, enough to last a lifetime. So you just have to find the island at the end of the rainbow, and then you can have the treasure—but only if you can catch the leprechaun guarding the gold."

"Just *one* leprechaun?" whispered Brendan. "I bet the two of us could catch him easily. Let's go to that island and find the gold."

His grandfather laughed. "If only it was as easy as that, my boy! Come now, it's getting late. Go to sleep—and sweet dreams."

"I'll dream of the golden treasure," whispered Brendan. "I'll dream of how it would be if . . ."

The next morning Grandpa heard Brendan cry out, "Grandpa! Come quick!"

Brendan stood pointing at the sky. There was a rainbow arching high above the sea, and the end of the rainbow came down on an island.

"There, see that? It's just like your story!" cried Brendan. "And it will be easy to get there. We can row across!"

"But it's just a fairy tale, my boy!" said Grandpa. "There's nothing over there but wind and sand."

"And a leprechaun guarding a pot full of gold," said Brendan. "Oh, please, Grandpa, let's try!"

He begged and begged until his grandfather got their rubber boots and hauled the heavy boat over the shingle into the surf.

Brendan quickly found their spades for digging peat and clambered into the boat.

The sea was still rough, and Grandpa had to row with all his might to make any headway against the current.

Every stroke of the oars, however, brought them a little closer
to the island.

"Nearly there!" cried Brendan, and then he heard the boat grating over the sand, and they jumped ashore.

"It must be here," whispered Brendan. "Do you see that elder tree? You always told me a leprechaun lives under every elder."

"But that is just a fairy tale," insisted Grandpa.
"It *could* be true," said Brendan, and he began to dig.

He dug down, deeper and deeper, all around the elder tree, and he found . . . nothing.

But while he was still digging, new elder bushes grew out of the sand, and now the island seemed to be a whole wood of elder trees and bushes.

Brendan and his grandfather dug and dug until evening came. Then Grandpa said, "It's late. Time to go home."

"You were right," said Brendan. "The story was only a fairy tale after all. But I wish it had been true."

Brendan and his grandfather headed down to their boat. All of a sudden, something flitted past Grandpa's head. Startled, Grandpa snatched it from the air. It was only the size of a squirrel, but it looked human, and it said politely, "Please let me go."

"Oh, of course," replied Grandpa, releasing the tiny creature. "I'm sorry, it's just that you startled me so."

The little creature chuckled. "I know, I know. The two of you have been looking for the gold, haven't you? You almost had it, too, if only you hadn't let me go!" The leprechaun laughed merrily. "Oh, I *am* a fortunate fellow to have been caught by the likes of you!"

With these words he suddenly climbed up on Grandpa's shoulder, tweaked the old man's nose, and chuckled, and the next moment he disappeared into the dark.

"My head's spinning!" whispered Brendan.

"Mine too," said Grandpa, dipping his oars in the water. But no sooner had he rowed a few strokes than the moon broke through the clouds, and the boat glided gently away down a silvery path to the shore, as if drawn along by a magical hand.

"This is lovely," said Brendan softly.

"You know, I don't really mind about not finding the gold," said Brendan as they climbed the steps to their house. "It was enough just to see a real leprechaun."

"It was indeed," said Grandpa, nodding. "And it wouldn't have been right to take his gold."

That night they slept soundly, until far into the next day, when the cow began to moo in her cow shed.

"Leave it to me," said Brendan, yawning. "I'll milk her."

He made his way barefoot over the yard to the cow shed. And then he could hardly believe his eyes: There stood the cow, with a little calf. There were a couple of chickens scratching about the yard too, and a fat pig grunting beside them.

"Grandpa!" shouted Brendan. "Come quick!"

Grandpa was already standing in the doorway, staring in astonishment at the bottle in his hand.

"I found this on the kitchen table," he said. "It's full of elderberry juice, and no matter how much you drink, it never gets any less."

Brendan and his grandfather smiled at each other. Then they went down to the beach and looked out at the island.

"Thank you!" called Brendan softly. And they heard, echoing back over the sea, "Thank *you!*"

First published in the United States, Great Britain, Canada,
Australia, and New Zealand in 1997 by North-South Books,
an imprint of Nord-Süd Verlag AG, Gossau Zürich, Switzerland.
Distributed in the United States by North-South Books Inc., New York.

Library of Congress Cataloging-in-Publication Data is available.
A CIP catalogue record for this book is available from The British Library.
ISBN 1-55858-692-X (trade binding)
1 3 5 7 9 TB 10 8 6 4 2
ISBN 1-55858-693-8 (library binding)
1 3 5 7 9 LB 10 8 6 4 2
Printed in Belgium

For more information about our books, and the authors and artists
who create them, visit our web site: http://www.northsouth.com